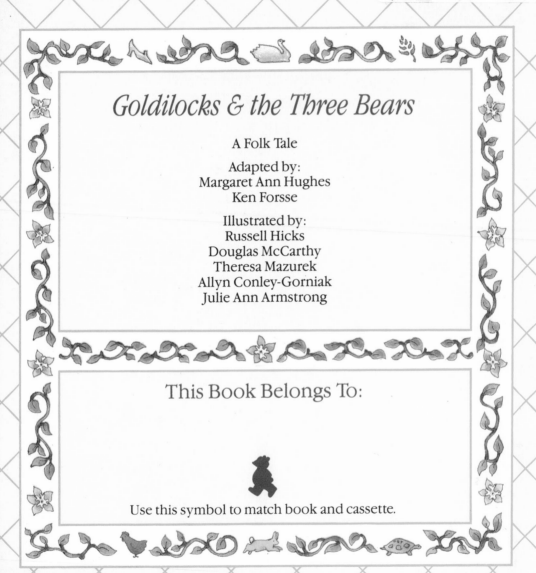

Goldilocks & the Three Bears

A Folk Tale

Adapted by:
Margaret Ann Hughes
Ken Forsse

Illustrated by:
Russell Hicks
Douglas McCarthy
Theresa Mazurek
Allyn Conley-Gorniak
Julie Ann Armstrong

This Book Belongs To:

Use this symbol to match book and cassette.

Once upon a time in a little cottage in a far off corner of the woods, there lived three bears…a Papa Bear, a Mama Bear and a Baby Bear.

Now the Papa Bear was a GREAT BIG bear.

The Mama Bear was a MEDIUM-SIZED bear.

And the Baby Bear was a LITTLE TINY bear.

The bears liked things that just fit them, so everything in the house was either BIG for Papa Bear, MEDIUM-SIZED for Mama Bear or TINY for the Baby Bear.

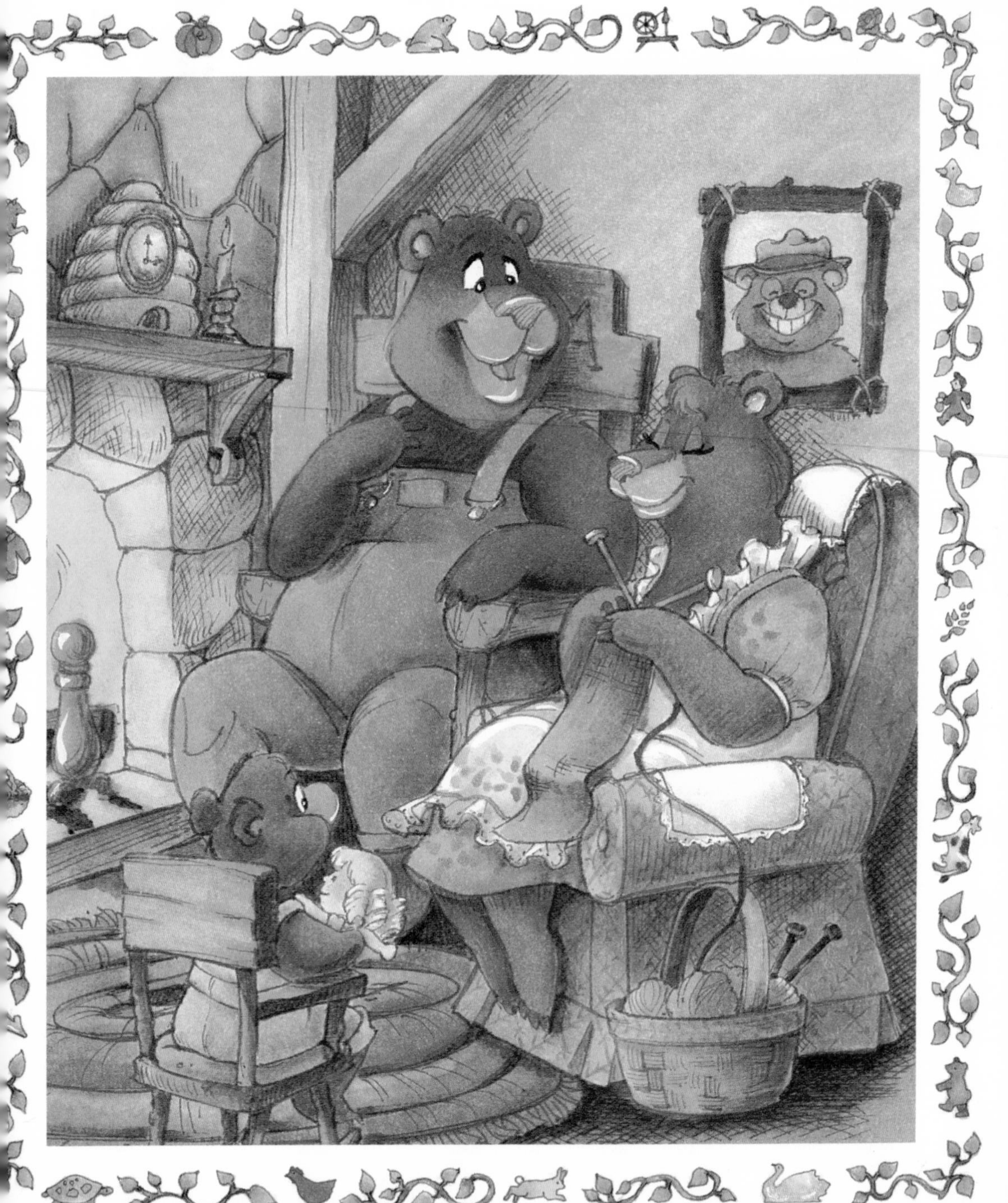

Now one morning, Mama Bear had just made a nice pot of porridge for breakfast. She suggested that they go out for their morning walk and see if they could find some honey to put on the porridge.

Mama Bear filled their bowls with porridge so it would cool while they went for their walk in the woods. And so they took up their empty honey pots, just in case they found some honey...and left on their walk.

Now on that same morning, a little girl was playing in the woods. Her name was Goldilocks.

As she came to a clearing in the woods, she saw the little cottage of the three bears.

She knocked on the door and waited for someone to answer.

When no one answered the door, Goldilocks opened the door and went right in.

Goldilocks looked around the room. There were three chairs by a nice warm fire, and three bowls of porridge on the table.

Goldilocks invited herself to sit at the table. Then she picked up Papa Bear's spoon and helped herself to a big bite of porridge from the GREAT BIG bowl.

Papa Bear's porridge was too hot. Then she took a great big bite from the MEDIUM-SIZED bowl.

Mama Bear's porridge was too cold. Then Goldilocks took a great big bite from the LITTLE TINY bowl.

Baby Bear's porridge was just the right temperature. And so Goldilocks ate up all the porridge in the LITTLE TINY bowl.

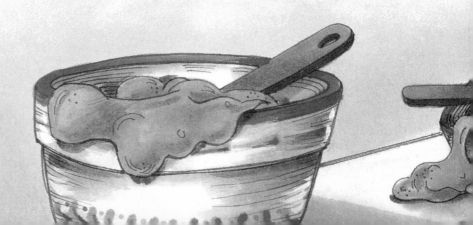

Then she noticed the three chairs by the nice warm fire.

Goldilocks climbed up into the GREAT BIG chair. It was all made of wood, and it had the name "PAPA" carved into the back of it. But the chair was so slippery and hard that Goldilocks slipped right out of it onto the floor!

Goldilocks brushed herself off, then she climbed into the MEDIUM-SIZED chair. It was a big overstuffed chair…and she sank deep into the cushions.

Goldilocks pushed and she scooted, and she scooted and pushed her way to the edge of the soft chair, until finally she managed to climb out.

Then she went to the LITTLE TINY chair. It was a rocking chair with a small cushion on the seat. She sat down in the chair.

Goldilocks rocked and rocked and rocked, but she rocked too hard...until she tipped over backwards! And the LITTLE TINY chair was broken all to pieces.

Goldilocks brushed herself off again, and, without a care, walked away from the broken chair. Then she looked about the room for something else to do, when she noticed a stairway leading upstairs. She climbed the stairs and came to a room with three beds, all nice and neatly made.

Then, as if she hadn't been naughty enough already, Goldilocks climbed into the GREAT BIG bed to take a nap.

Papa Bear's bed was too hard, so Goldilocks scooted herself off of it. Then she climbed into the MEDIUM-SIZED bed. But that bed was so soft that Goldilocks sank into it like a cherry sinks into whipped cream.

Goldilocks rolled first one way, and then the other, until finally, after several tries, she managed to roll out of Mama Bear's bed. Then she climbed into the LITTLE TINY bed.

Goldilocks liked the LITTLE TINY bed best of all. So she cuddled deep beneath the blankets and fell fast asleep.

By and by, the three bears came home with their honey pots full of honey.

Just then, the bears saw the spoons in their bowls, which meant that someone had been there…eating their porridge!

The Baby Bear was very sad that someone had eaten all his porridge. That left him with nothing to eat for breakfast…and he was so hungry.

It was then that Papa Bear noticed that his chair had been moved closer to the fire.

Mama Bear and Papa Bear indeed discovered that someone had been sitting in their chairs. Then Baby Bear ran to the pieces of wood that were once his chair.

The Baby Bear cried and cried over his broken chair. He had loved to rock back and forth, back and forth, while Papa Bear told him stories. But now there was no chair left.

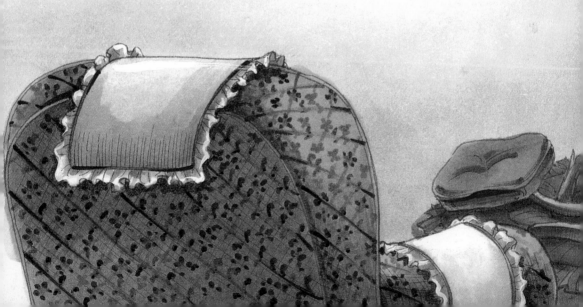

Papa Bear sniffed the air and decided to go upstairs to see if anything else was out of order. It wasn't long before he noticed his unmade bed.

Then Mama Bear saw from the mussed blankets that someone had been sleeping in her bed, too.

Baby Bear saw Goldilocks sleeping soundly in his
LITTLE TINY bed. The three bears quietly tip-
toed to the bed and looked down upon the sleeping
little girl.

Goldilocks woke up and rubbed her eyes hard, just in case she might be dreaming. But no…she wasn't. There, standing around her, were three very angry-looking bears!

All of a sudden, Goldilocks realized that she had made a big mistake by entering their home uninvited. And she was very frightened.

Goldilocks tried to explain, but she was so afraid, they were bears after all, that she jumped from the bed and ran out the door into the woods.

The three bears did not chase after Goldilocks. They knew she had learned a very important lesson and would never go uninvited into anyone's house again.

Mama Bear poured Baby Bear a new bowl of porridge. And then the three bears sat down to their breakfast of porridge…with honey on it.

nd they all lived happily ever after.